CU00869406

Translated from Dutch by Polly Lawson
First published in English in 1997 by Floris Books, 15 Harrison Gardens, Edinburgh.
© 1997 Christofoor Publishers, Zeist. English version © Floris Books 1997
British Library CIP Data available   ISBN 0-86315-254-6   Printed in Belgium

Dora Duck and the Juicy Pears

A story by Evelien van Dort
Illustrated by Marjan van Zeyl

Floris Books

Dora Duck lives on the farm with her family. Every day they swim in the stream.

They're very hungry today, but there isn't enough food to eat.
The ducks start to squabble over a nice piece of weed.

"Let's go and look somewhere else for food," says Dora. And off they go.

The ducks soon become lost in the long meadow grass.

They meet two frogs in the meadow. The frogs will know the way to the stream.

"We're lost and hungry," says Dora. "Please help us find the stream."

"It's this way, follow us," croak the frogs. And jump through the grass as fast as they can go.

But Dora is looking the other way. And wanders off by herself.

Dora soon arrives in front of the farmhouse. She is almost
home! Hurrying along, she trips
and falls. She lands with
her beak on a strange
green fruit.

She takes a bite of the fruit. Mmmm, it tastes delicious! It's a sweet juicy pear. Then she hears children's voices.

It's the farmer's children collecting the pears. And there are the other ducks gathering around!

"Look," says Sally. "The ducks have been eating our pears." The ducks think the children are cross with them, and they rush away back to the stream.

"I didn't know ducks liked pears," says Billy. "Let's share the pears with them." The children fill a basin with juicy pears and carry it down to the stream. They leave the pears on the bank.

The ducks are still hungry and feeling sorry for themselves.
Then Dora sees the pears on the bank. What a surprise!

The ducks start to eat up the pears. They're delicious! The children watch happily from the window.

Dora Duck and her family waddle back to the stream, contented and full.